Blanket

by Ruth Ohi

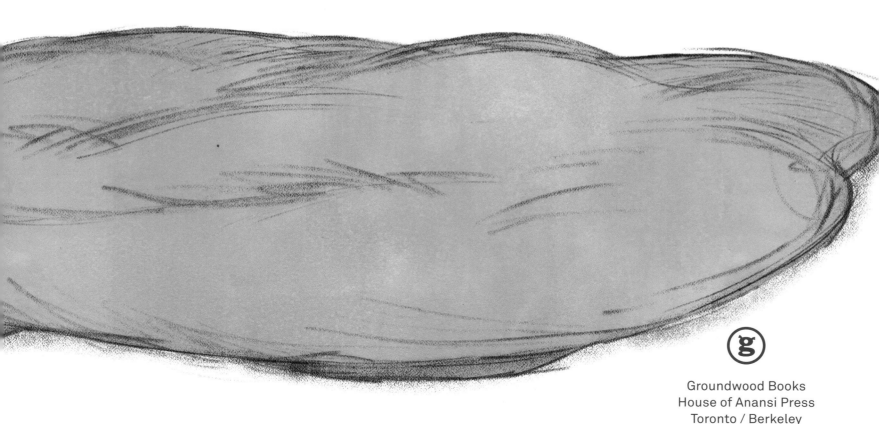

Groundwood Books
House of Anansi Press
Toronto / Berkeley

Published in 2022 by Groundwood Books / House of Anansi Press
groundwoodbooks.com

We gratefully acknowledge the Canada Council for the Arts, the Ontario Arts Council and the Government of Canada for their financial support of our publishing program.

Canada Council   Conseil des Arts
for the Arts   du Canada

ONTARIO ARTS COUNCIL
CONSEIL DES ARTS DE L'ONTARIO
an Ontario government agency
un organisme du gouvernement de l'Ontario

With the participation of the Government of Canada
Avec la participation du gouvernement du Canada | Canadä

Library and Archives Canada Cataloguing in Publication
Title: Blanket / Ruth Ohi.
Names: Ohi, Ruth, author, illustrator.
Identifiers: Canadiana (print) 20210338172 | Canadiana (ebook) 20210338180 | ISBN 9781773066141 (hardcover) | ISBN 9781773066158 (EPUB) | ISBN 9781773066165 (Kindle)
Subjects: LCSH: Stories without words. | LCGFT: Wordless picture books.
Classification: LCC PS8579.H47 B53 2022 | DDC jC813/.6—dc23

Edited by Karen Li and Emma Sakamoto
Designed by Michael Solomon
Printed and bound in South Korea

For Annie, Sara & K

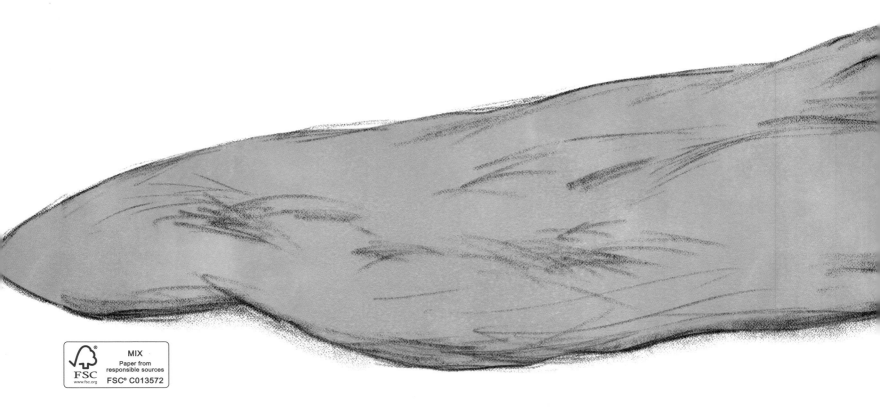

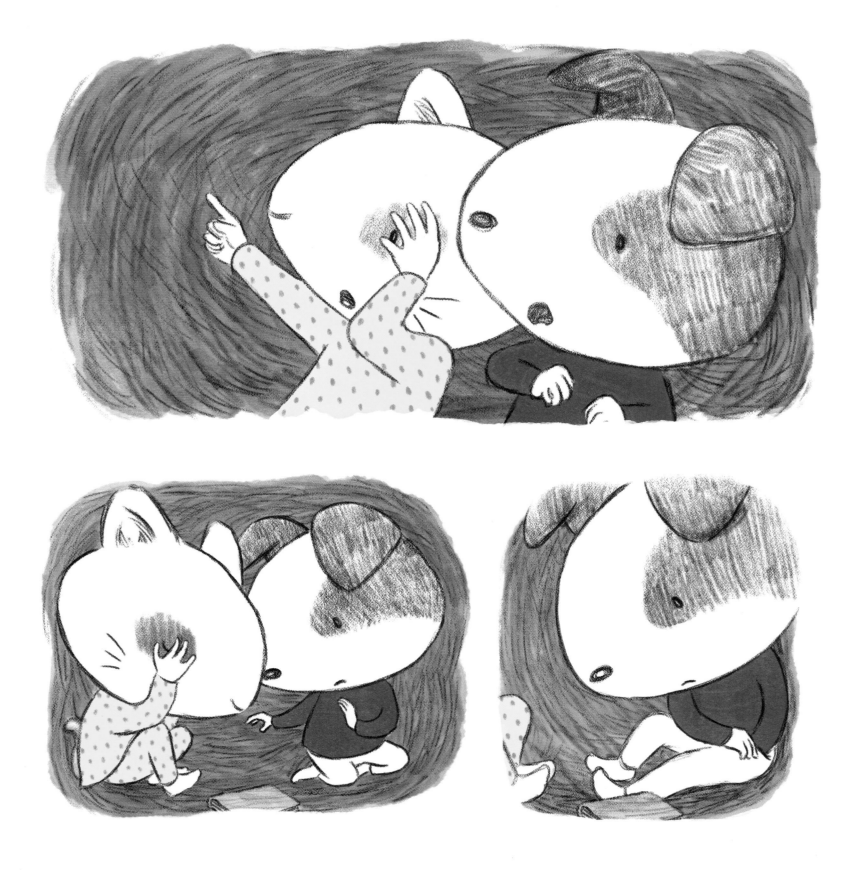

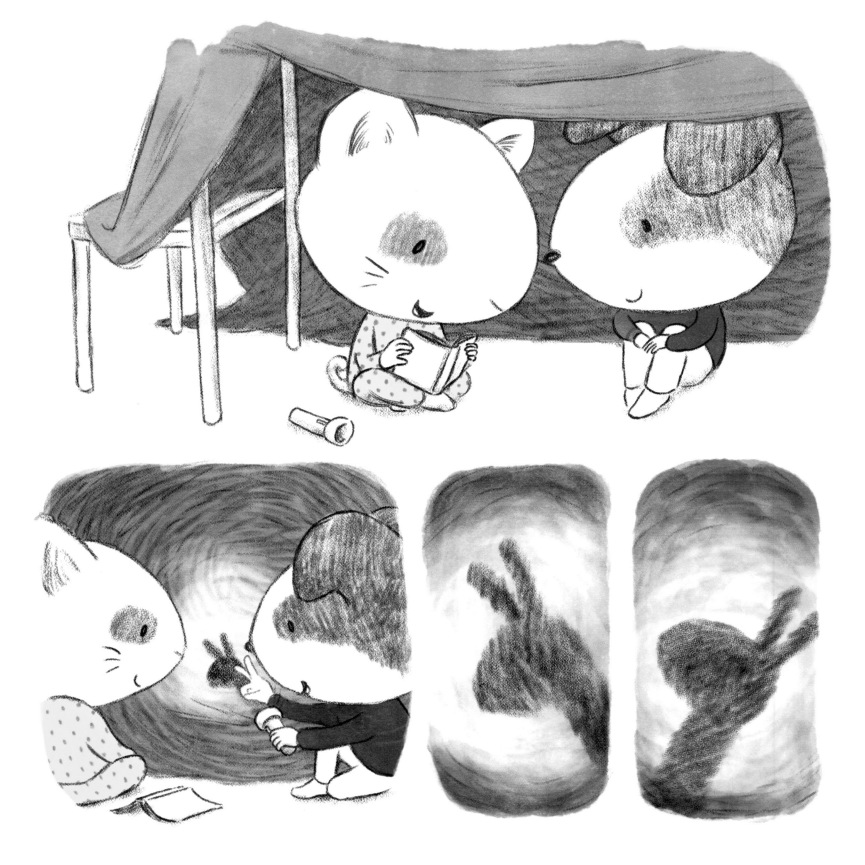

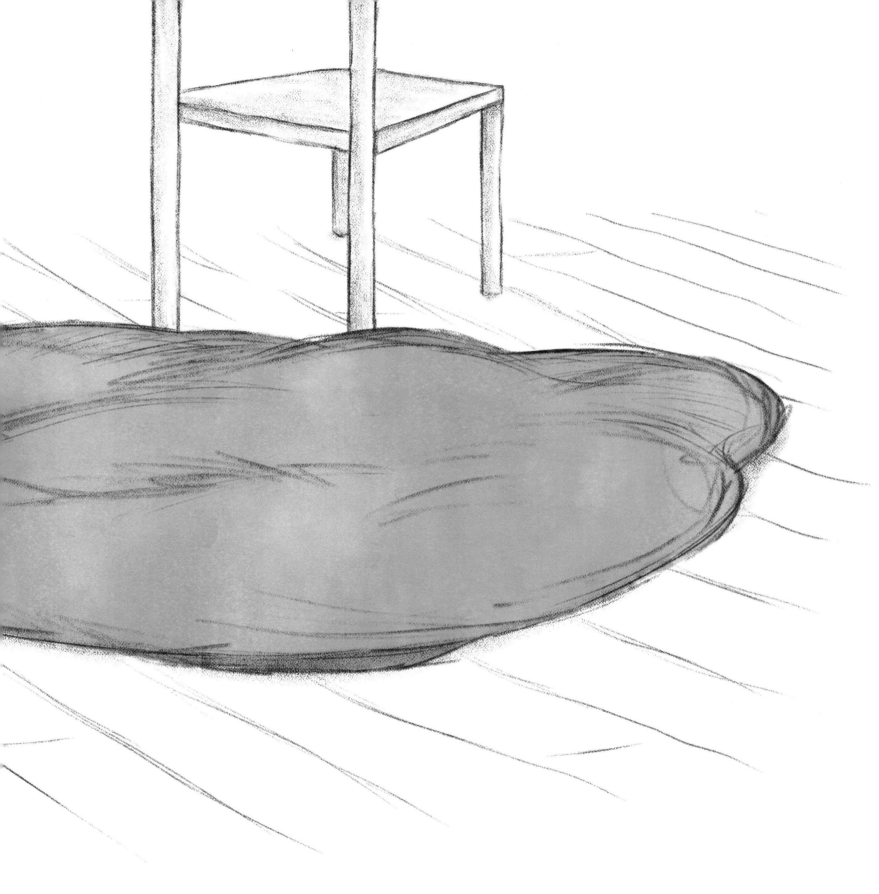

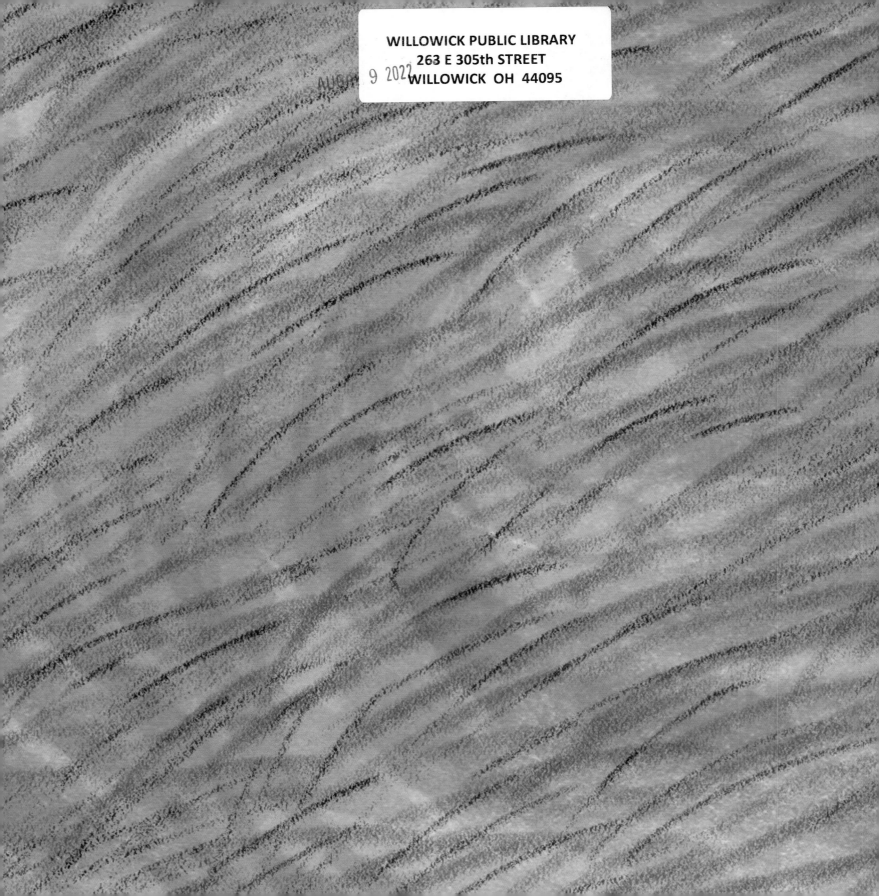